I can't bear
to be
without
my books.

This Book Belongs To

Elsie Wall.

The
Fairy Tale
Book

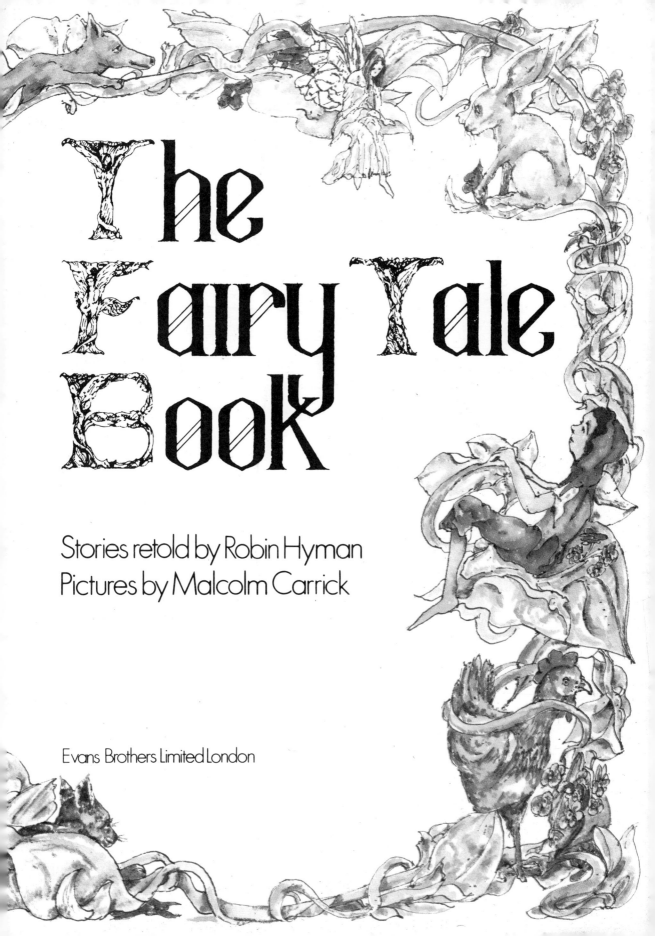

The Fairy Tale Book

Stories retold by Robin Hyman
Pictures by Malcolm Carrick

Evans Brothers Limited London

Published by Evans Brothers Limited,
Montague House, Russell Square,
London, WC1B 5BX

First published 1974

Set in Monotype Baskerville
and printed in Great Britain by
Hazell Watson & Viney Ltd,
Aylesbury, Bucks

ISBN 0 237 44787 8   PRA 4040

Contents

The Little Red Hen

A pig, a duck, a cat and and a Little Red Hen lived in a house. While the pig wallowed and the duck swam and the cat slept happily in the sun, the Little Red Hen did all the housework.

One day the Little Red Hen found a grain of wheat.
"Who will plant it?" she asked the pig, the duck and the cat.
All they said was, "Not I."
So the Little Red Hen planted it herself.

The grain of wheat grew and grew until it was ready to cut.
"Who will cut it?" the Little Red Hen asked the pig, the duck and the cat.
All they said was, "Not I."
So the Little Red Hen cut it herself, with her sharp beak.

7

When the wheat was cut the Little Red Hen said, "Who will take it to the mill?"

But the pig, the duck and the cat said, "Not I."

So the Little Red Hen took the wheat to the mill herself.

Soon the miller brought the sack of flour back from the mill.
"Who will make the flour into bread?" asked the Little Red Hen.
The pig, the duck and the cat said, "Not I."
So the Little Red Hen made the bread herself.

When the Little Red Hen had
baked the bread she took the
lovely crusty loaf out of the oven.

"Who will eat the bread?" she
asked.
"I will," said the pig,
the duck and the cat.

"No, you won't," said the Little Red Hen. "I found it and I planted it
and I cut it and I took it to the mill and I baked it. Now I am going to
eat it all up myself."
And that's what she did.

Goldilocks and the Three Bears

Once upon a time there were three bears. The Daddy was a great big bear, the Mummy was a middle-sized bear, and the Baby was a tiny little bear.

One day Mummy Bear made some porridge. It was too hot to eat so the three bears left it on the table and went for a walk in the woods until it cooled down.

While they were out, a little girl called Goldilocks knocked at the door of the house. There was no answer. The door was open and Goldilocks walked in.

She saw the lovely porridge standing on the table. "I'll taste it," she said.

First she tasted the Daddy Bear's porridge which was in a great big bowl. It was too hot. Then she tasted Mummy Bear's porridge which was in a middle-sized bowl. It was too cold. Then she tasted Baby Bear's porridge which was in a tiny little bowl. It was just right, so she gobbled it all up.

Goldilocks saw the chairs in the room and sat down on the great big chair, but it was too large. Next she sat on the middle-sized chair, but it was still too big. So she sat on the tiny little chair. This time she was too heavy for the chair, and it broke into pieces.

Then Goldilocks felt tired, so she went upstairs to have a rest. First she lay down on Daddy Bear's great big bed, but it was too hard. Then she lay down on Mummy Bear's middle-sized bed, but it was too soft. So she tried the Baby Bear's tiny little bed.

It was just right, and she fell asleep.

Soon the three bears came back from their walk ready to eat their porridge.

"Someone's been tasting my porridge," said Daddy Bear in his great big voice.

"Someone's been tasting my porridge," said Mummy Bear in her middle-sized voice.

"Someone's been tasting my porridge," said Baby Bear in his tiny little voice, "and they've eaten it all up!"

"Someone's been sitting on my chair," said Daddy Bear in his great big voice.

"Someone's been sitting on my chair," said Mummy Bear in her middle-sized voice.

"Someone's been sitting on my chair," said Baby Bear in his tiny little voice, "and it's fallen to pieces!"

Then they went upstairs.

"Someone's been lying on my bed," said Daddy Bear, in his great big voice.

"Someone's been lying on my bed," said Mummy Bear in her middle-sized voice.

"Someone's been lying on my bed," said Baby Bear in his tiny little voice, "and here she is!"

Just then Goldilocks woke up and was frightened to see the three bears. She leapt out of bed, rushed down the stairs and back to her own house.

And from that day to this the three bears have not seen her again.

The Turnip

One day a farmer planted a little turnip. It grew into an enormous turnip—so large that the farmer could not pull it up. So he called his wife to help him.

The farmer's wife pulled the farmer, and the farmer pulled the enormous turnip. But still they could not pull it up. So the farmer's wife called her granddaughter.

The grand-daughter pulled the farmer's wife, the farmer's wife pulled the farmer, and the farmer pulled the enormous turnip. But still they could not pull it up. So the grand-daughter called the dog.

The dog pulled the grand-daughter, the grand-daughter pulled the farmer's wife, the farmer's wife pulled the farmer, and the farmer pulled the enormous turnip. But still they could not pull it up. So the dog called the cat.

The cat pulled the dog, the dog pulled the grand-daughter, the grand-daughter pulled the farmer's wife, the farmer's wife pulled the farmer, and the farmer pulled the enormous turnip. But still they could not pull it up. So the cat called the mouse.

The mouse pulled the cat, the cat pulled the dog, the dog pulled the grand-daughter, the grand-daughter pulled the farmer's wife, the farmer's wife pulled the farmer, and the farmer pulled the enormous turnip. And suddenly they all toppled over backwards. They'd pulled the enormous turnip right out of the ground!

17

The Hare and the Tortoise

"You're very, very slow," the hare said to the tortoise who was crawling along.

"If we have a race, I'm sure I will beat you," said the tortoise, and the hare burst out laughing.

They agreed to have a race and other animals came to watch. The fox was the judge.

"Ready, steady, go!" the fox shouted to the hare and the tortoise.

Off they went and soon the hare was far ahead. The tortoise crawled along slowly behind.

The hare was so far in front that he thought he had time for a rest.

He lay down by a tree and was soon fast asleep.

Slowly and steadily the tortoise crept along. At last he crawled right past the hare, who was still sleeping under the tree.

Suddenly the hare woke up but he was too late to catch up the tortoise. The tortoise had won the race.

The Three Little Pigs

Three little pigs left the pig-sty where they lived. Winter was coming and they wanted to build a house of their own.

The first little pig found some straw and built a house with it.

When the house was finished a big bad wolf came along.

"Can I come in?" he asked.

"No," said the frightened little pig.

"Then I'll huff and I'll puff and I'll blow your house down," said the big bad wolf.

And that's what he did.

The second pig found some twigs and built a house with them in the freezing cold beside the river.

When the house was finished, a big bad wolf came along.

"Can I come in?" he asked.

"No," said the frightened little pig.

"Then I'll huff and I'll puff and I'll blow your house down," said the big bad wolf.

And that's what he did.

The third little pig found some bricks and built a house with them.

When he had finished, along came a big bad wolf.
"Can I come in?" he asked.

"No," said the frightened little pig.
"Then I'll huff and I'll puff and I'll blow your house down," said the big bad wolf.
This time the house did not fall down.

The wolf was very angry. He thought of a plan to get into the pig's strong brick house. So he jumped on to the roof of the house and tried to climb down the chimney.

24

But the little pig was too clever. The wolf crashed down the chimney and fell into a big pot of boiling water. And that was the end of the big bad wolf.

The little pig was kind and he asked the two other little pigs to come and live with him in his strong brick house. And all three pigs lived happily ever after.

The Gingerbread Boy

One day a little old woman made a gingerbread cake that looked like a boy. She made a jacket out of chocolate, and eyes out of two big currants. Then she put it in the oven to cook.

When she opened the oven door, out jumped a gingerbread boy. Suddenly he rushed into the street and ran away.

The old woman chased him but he shouted:
"Run, run as fast as you can!
You can't catch me,
I'm the gingerbread man."

The little gingerbread boy ran on and on.

A cow saw him and said, "You look nice, I want to eat you."

But the gingerbread boy said, "I have run away from a little old woman and I can run away from you too." And he shouted to the cow:

"Run, run as fast as you can!

You can't catch me,

I'm the gingerbread man."

The little gingerbread boy saw a horse in a field.

"You look nice. I want to eat you," said the horse.

"I have run away from a little old woman and from a cow and I can run away from you too," said the gingerbread boy.

And he shouted to the horse:
"Run, run as fast as you can!
You can't catch me,
I'm the gingerbread man."

The little gingerbread boy ran on and on until he saw a bear.

"You look nice, I want to eat you," said the bear.

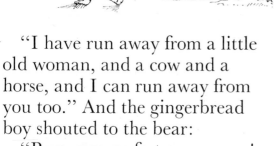

"I have run away from a little old woman, and a cow and a horse, and I can run away from you too." And the gingerbread boy shouted to the bear:
"Run, run, as fast as you can!
You can't catch me,
I'm the gingerbread man."

At last the gingerbread boy saw a fox and shouted to him, "You can't catch me."

But the fox was clever.

"I don't want to," he said with a smile.

Soon the gingerbread boy came to a river. He wanted to cross over but he couldn't swim.

"Jump on my tail and I will take you across the river," said the fox.

The fox started swimming across the river with the gingerbread boy on his tail. "Jump on my back or you may fall off," said the fox.

Then the fox said, "Jump on my head, or you may fall in the water."

And then he said, "Jump on my nose."

When they got to the other side of the river the fox threw back his head. The gingerbread boy fell into his mouth and the fox gobbled him up.

And that was the end of the gingerbread boy.

The Lion and the Mouse

The big, strong lion was fast asleep. Suddenly he woke up. A tiny mouse had disturbed his sleep, and the lion was very angry.

"Please don't hurt me," said the frightened mouse. "I didn't mean to annoy you." And the lion let him go.

"Thank you, lion," said the mouse. "One day I may be able to help you."

The lion laughed at such a ridiculous idea.

But some time later the lion was caught in a net. He tried hard to get out but he couldn't.

When the mouse heard the lion roaring, he scampered along to help. With his sharp teeth he bit at the ropes until they broke.

The lion was free. "Thank you, mouse," he said, "I won't ever laugh at you again."

Cinderella

There was once a beautiful girl called Cinderella who had two ugly sisters. They were always unkind to Cinderella. They made her do all the hard work in the house, and she had no nice clothes.

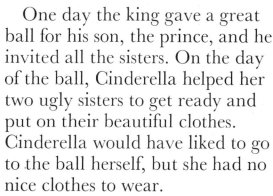

One day the king gave a great ball for his son, the prince, and he invited all the sisters. On the day of the ball, Cinderella helped her two ugly sisters to get ready and put on their beautiful clothes. Cinderella would have liked to go to the ball herself, but she had no nice clothes to wear.

When her sisters had gone and Cinderella was alone she burst into tears. Suddenly there was a knock at the door. It was her fairy godmother.

"Would you like to go to the ball?" she asked.

"Of course," said Cinderella sadly, "but I've only got rags to wear."

The fairy godmother waved her magic wand and Cinderella found she was dressed in lovely clothes. The fairy godmother waved her wand again and a pumpkin changed into a beautiful coach and horses to take her to the ball.

"Off you go," the fairy godmother said, "but you must be back here by the last stroke of midnight—or the magic spell will be broken."

As soon as Cinderella arrived at the ball, the Prince saw how beautiful she was and he danced with her all the evening.

"Who can that lovely girl be?" everybody wondered, including the two ugly sisters, who did not recognise Cinderella in her new clothes.

Cinderella enjoyed herself so much that she forgot what time it was. Suddenly she heard the clock striking twelve. It was midnight. She rushed straight out of the ballroom without saying goodbye to anyone—not even to the charming Prince.

On her way down the stairs, she dropped one of her slippers.

The Prince saw it and picked it up.

Meanwhile Cinderella was not home until after midnight, so the magic spell was broken. Her coach and beautiful clothes disappeared and she was dressed in rags again.

The day after the ball the Prince and his friends looked everywhere for the girl whose foot fitted the shoe he had found.

Then one of the men called at the house where Cinderella and her ugly sisters lived. The sisters tried on the shoe but it did not fit.

Then Cinderella said, "Can I try it on?" and she did, while the sisters sat and laughed. To their amazement, the shoe fitted Cinderella perfectly.

The Prince's search was over. Cinderella was driven in a lovely carriage to meet the Prince again. And soon they got married and lived happily ever after.

The Elves and the Shoemaker

There was once a shoemaker who worked hard but he was very, very poor. He only had enough leather left to make one pair of shoes. So in the evening he cut out the leather ready to make his last pair of shoes the next morning. Then he went to bed.

The shoemaker and his wife came down in the morning and they were amazed to find that, in the night, a fine pair of shoes had been made out of the leather.

The shoes were so well made that the shoemaker sold them for more money than the usual price. With the money, the shoemaker bought enough leather for two pairs of shoes.

And before he went to bed that night he cut out the leather ready to make two pairs of shoes the next day.

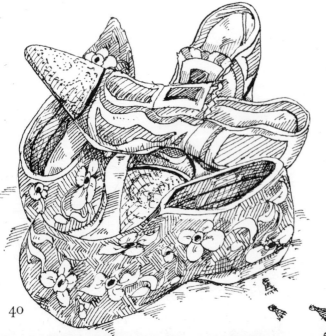

In the morning they found the same thing had happened again. This time two fine pairs of shoes had been made. And so it went on night after night.

At last the shoemaker and his wife stayed up one night to see what happened.

As the clock struck midnight the door opened. They were amazed to see two elves come in and start making the shoes. The elves worked fast and as soon as they had finished they went away again.

When the elves had gone the shoemaker said to his wife, "How can we thank them for all they have done for us?"

The wife had an idea. She made some lovely little clothes for the elves to wear, and the next night they left out the clothes for the elves to find.

The shoemaker and his wife hid behind the curtains and waited. And sure enough at midnight the elves came in as usual to make the shoes. They saw all the little clothes spread out. They were so delighted that they put the clothes on and then jumped on the table and started dancing. At last they went out of the house, singing and laughing happily.

And from that day to this, the shoemaker and his wife have never seen the elves again. But now, thanks to the elves, the shoemaker and his wife are no longer poor and they have lived happily ever since.

Little Red Riding Hood

A pretty girl lived in the country. She always wore a red cape and red hood, so people called her Little Red Riding Hood.

One day her mother said to her, "Grandmother is not very well, so please go and see her and take her this basket of cake and fruit."

Little Red Riding Hood set off to visit her grandmother. She lived on the other side of the wood.

As she walked happily through the wood, Little Red Riding Hood met a wolf.

"Where are you going with that basket?" said the wolf.

"I'm going to see my grandmother who's not very well," said Little Red Riding Hood.

The clever wolf had an idea. He ran ahead of Little Red Riding Hood and knocked on the door of Grandmother's house. But Grandmother had seen the wolf coming and hid in a cupboard and locked the door.

The wolf climbed into the house. He put on Grandmother's nightdress and got into her bed.

Soon Little Red Riding Hood knocked at the door.

"Come in," said the wolf, pretending to be Grandmother.

"Oh, Grandmother, what big bright eyes you have," said Little Red Riding Hood.

"All the better to see you with," said the wolf.

"Oh, Grandmother, what big ears you have," said Little Red Riding Hood.

"All the better to hear you with," said the wolf.

"Oh, Grandmother, what great big teeth you have," said Little Red Riding Hood.

"All the better to eat you with," said the wolf.

Suddenly the wolf leapt out of bed.
Little Red Riding Hood screamed.
Luckily a woodman heard her, rushed into the house and saved her from the wolf.

The wolf ran out of the house,
and the woodman chased him
away.

And Little Red Riding Hood walked back to her own home and she
never saw another wolf again.

The Ant and the Grasshopper

One day in the autumn an ant was getting some little bits of food to save up for the cold winter.

A grasshopper passed by looking sad and hungry. "Can I have some food?" he begged the ant.

"What have you been doing while I have been working hard?" asked the ant.

"I've been so busy singing, I didn't have time to collect food for the winter," said the grasshopper.

The ant said, "If you've been singing all the summer, then you can dance all the winter!"

Jack and the Beanstalk

There was once a poor lady who lived with her son Jack. All they had in the world was one cow, which did not give much milk.

So Jack went to the market to sell the cow. On the way he met a man who said, "I'll give you five magic coloured beans in exchange for your cow. You plant the beans tonight, and they'll grow right up to the sky by morning. If they don't you can have your cow back!"

Jack took the beans home.
"How much money did you sell
the cow for?" his mother asked.
"For five beans," Jack said.
His mother was very angry.
"We needed some money," she
said and threw the beans out of
the window.

Jack went sadly to bed. When he
woke up in the morning and
looked out, he saw that an
enormous beanstalk had grown
right up past the window.
He jumped out of the window
on to the beanstalk and climbed
and climbed, high up into the sky.

Suddenly he saw a castle.

Jack walked over to the castle and saw a tall lady.

"I am very hungry. Can I have something to eat, please?" Jack asked the lady.

"Beware of my husband, the Giant. If he sees you he'll eat you up," said the lady, but she gave him some food.

Just then they heard the Giant come in.

"Quick, go and hide," the lady said to Jack.

53

Jack hid in the oven while the Giant ate his enormous dinner and counted his gold. Then the Giant fell asleep, snoring loudly.

Jack crept out of the oven, took a bagful of the Giant's gold, and ran out of the castle.

He went down the beanstalk as fast as he could go. His mother was delighted to see him again.

They lived happily until the money was all spent. Then Jack decided to climb up the beanstalk again and he went back to the Giant's castle.

This time Jack saw that in front of the Giant was a hen. Each time the Giant said "Lay", the hen laid a golden egg. When the Giant fell asleep snoring, Jack took the hen and went home down the beanstalk with it.

After a while he said to his mother, "I want to have another adventure. I must climb the beanstalk just once more."

This time the Giant was listening to a golden harp which played music to him. Soon the Giant and his wife were fast asleep.

Jack crept up to the sleeping Giant and took the golden harp. He ran with it as fast as he could go to the top of the beanstalk.

When the Giant woke up he found that the harp was missing. He chased Jack and followed him down the beanstalk.

Jack got down to the ground safely just in time.

He picked up an axe and cut down the beanstalk as quickly as he could. It crashed to the ground with the Giant on it.

And after that Jack and his mother lived happily ever after with their golden eggs and the golden harp.

58

The Emperor's New Clothes

Once upon a time there was an Emperor who enjoyed wearing lovely clothes and showing them off to people more than anything else in the world. He changed his clothes many times each day. All the tailors in his kingdom worked day and night to make new clothes for him.

One day two men came to see him and said that they would like to make him some beautiful new clothes.

"They are very special," the men said, "because no one who is stupid will be able to see the clothes."

The Emperor asked the men to make the clothes quickly and gave them enough money to buy fine cloth.

But the men did not go and buy fine cloth or make any clothes. They just pretended.

The Emperor sent a man to see how they were getting on but, of course, he could not see any clothes. He could not say that he was unable to see anything or people would say he was stupid.

"How lovely," he said and went and told the Emperor.

Then the Emperor went to see for himself. He too could see nothing but he told the men, "Yes, they are very fine. I will wear these beautiful new clothes tomorrow."

The men pretended to work all night to get them ready in time. When they had finished and been paid for their work, they rushed away.

Everyone said, "How lovely the Emperor's new clothes are!"
They couldn't see anything, of course, but they were afraid to seem stupid.
Then suddenly a child said at the top of his voice, "He is not wearing anything."
The Emperor took no notice and went marching along the street wearing no clothes at all. All the people started to laugh.

The Boy and the Wolf

A boy was looking after some sheep. He sometimes got bored.

One day, just for fun, he ran into the village and shouted, "Wolf!"

All the people in the village rushed to help the boy but there was no wolf to be seen.

The boy did this again many
times. Each time the people
rushed out of the village to help
him but there was never a wolf to
be seen.

One day a wolf really came. The
boy shouted, "Wolf! Wolf!" but
this time no one believed him.
They all thought he was
pretending again. Nobody came to
help and the wolf carried off one
of the precious sheep. The people
in the village were very angry with
the boy. Never again did he cry
"Wolf!" just for fun.